To the wonderful Jo Anne Davies –
with massive thanks & much love

xxx

First published 2013 by Walker Books Ltd
87 Vauxhall Walk, London SE11 5HJ

2 4 6 8 10 9 7 5 3 1

Text © 2013 Vivian French
Illustrations © 2013 Jo Anne Davies

The right of Vivian French and Jo Anne Davies to be identified
as author and illustrator respectively of this work
has been asserted by them in accordance with the
Copyright, Designs and Patents Act 1988

This book has been typeset in StempelSchneidler

Printed and bound in Great Britain
by Clays Ltd, St Ives plc

British Library Cataloguing in Publication Data:
a catalogue record for this book is available from
the British Library

ISBN 978-1-4063-3342-8

www.walker.co.uk

# Stargirl Academy

# Sophie's
## Shining Spell

VIVIAN FRENCH

WALKER
BOOKS

# Stargirl Academy

## Where magic makes a difference!

**HEAD TEACHER**
*Fairy Mary McBee*

**DEPUTY HEAD**
*Miss Scritch*

**TEACHER**
*Fairy Fifibelle Lee*

# TEAM STARLIGHT

Lily

Madison

Sophie

Ava

Emma

Olivia

# TEAM TWINSTAR

Melody

Jackson

Dear Stargirl,

Welcome to *Stargirl Academy*!

My name is Fairy Mary McBee, and I'm delighted you're here. All my Stargirls are very special, and I can tell that you are wonderful too.

We'll be learning how to use magic safely and efficiently to help anyone who is in trouble, but before we go any further I have a request. The Academy MUST be kept secret. This is VERY important…

So may I ask you to join our other Stargirls in making The Promise? Read it – say it out loud if you wish – then sign your name on the bottom line.

Thank you so much … and well done!

*Fairy Mary*

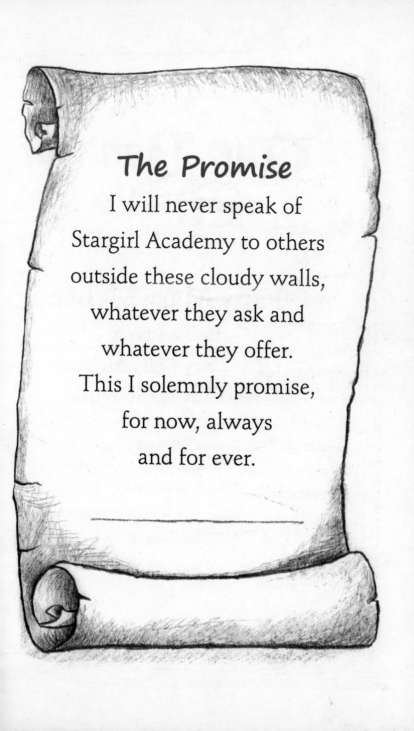

## The Promise

I will never speak of
Stargirl Academy to others
outside these cloudy walls,
whatever they ask and
whatever they offer.
This I solemnly promise,
for now, always
and for ever.

_____

# The Book of Spells

by
## Fairy Mary McBee

### Head Teacher at

### The Fairy Mary McBee

### Academy for Stargirls

◆ ◆ ◆

*A complete list of Spells can be obtained from the Academy.*

*Only the fully qualified need apply. Other applications*

*will be refused.*

# Shining Spells

Shining Spells may only be used by students who have won at least two stars. Any Shining Spell will require a higher level of concentration than a Shimmering Spell or a Starry Spell.

## Shining Spells include such spells as:

- Sliding warts, boils, spots etc from subject to subject [e.g. frogs, toads or human beings]
- Restoring music to damaged violins
- Pleasant dreams for the elderly

Hello! My name is Sophie Briggs. I live with my mum and my dad and Pete. Pete's younger than me, and if you've got a little brother you'll know how very, VERY annoying they can be. When he spilled orange juice all over Mum's not-very-new-but-she-still-loved-it coat, she said it was MY fault, because if I hadn't shouted at him he wouldn't have run down the hall and tripped.

I bet you'd have shouted at Pete too, though. He'd drawn aeroplanes all over the cover of my special notebook. It's lucky he can't read properly because — and PLEASE don't tell anyone! — that's the notebook where I write down everything I've learned after a day at Stargirl Academy.

It's TOTALLY secret and I've promised not to tell anybody about what we do.

The Academy used to be The Cloudy Towers Academy for Fairy Godmothers (I am NOT joking!) but then they decided that Fairy Godmothers were a bit old-fashioned, and now they teach girls to be Stargirls instead. We learn magic and spells so we can help people – really, truly help them. I don't think they'd ever let me use a spell to turn Pete into a frog, for instance. Well, not unless it would help him jump.

Actually, I think Pete might rather like being a frog – he's always bursting with energy. They closed the play park at the end of our road so I couldn't take him there any more, and that made him bouncier than ever. We haven't got a garden, so there's nowhere for him to pretend to be an aeroplane, which is what he likes best. When he tries to do it at home in our flat it drives us nuts.

Everyone round here is fed up that the park is shut. It was the only green space we had. It's dreadful without it, and I made a promise to myself the very first day I went to The Academy that if ever it was my turn to choose who to help it would be everyone in Greenberry Street!

Love Sophie

# Chapter One

I was watching TV with Pete when the Tingle came. Mum had popped out to get some bread, but Pete didn't want to go with her so I said I'd look after him. He'd said he was sorry about my notebook, and I'd said I was sorry for shouting at him, and he was sitting on the sofa beside me when suddenly there was this sharp pain in my elbow.

I jumped, and Pete looked at me in surprise. "Why did you jump?"

I couldn't tell him. I just said I'd got pins and needles. He always thinks that sounds funny, so he laughed and went on watching his programme.

I rubbed my elbow. The Tingle is like a

tiny electric shock and it means that it's time for Stargirl lessons. The Academy floats on a special kind of cloud, and when the Tingle comes, it means the cloud is nearby. The last two times I got the Tingle it went misty outside, and when I opened our door there was a path right in front of me leading straight to the Academy. The first time I walked down it I was REALLY nervous; I had no idea what I was going to find. If anyone had told me I'd end up in The Fairy Mary McBee Academy for Stargirls, I would never EVER have believed them.

But now I was used to going, and I couldn't wait to go back and see all the others in Team Starlight. There are six of us, and we have such fun together! Melody and Jackson are there as well, but they sometimes want to do stuff on their own. They call themselves Team Twinstar. They're OK, though ... well, most of the time. But my team is fabulous, and we do SUCH interesting things.

It's brilliant to spend time learning magic and spells. We've learnt two already: a Shimmering Spell and a Starry Spell. One taught us how to float things and the other how to solidify them. We can only use the spells when we're having a Stargirl day, but it makes me feel very special to know that I can actually do a little magic.

There's another amazing thing about the Academy, and it took me ages to believe it could really be true ... but it is! Even though you feel as if you've had a whole day away from home, nobody knows you've gone, because when you get back it's EXACTLY the same time as when you left. Isn't that extraordinary? Madison says she thinks our head teacher has some magic way of squashing time up so it works differently in different places. Madison likes to ask loads of questions, but when I think about things like that my head hurts. I just feel happy it's all OK and Mum doesn't have to worry that I've gone missing or run away from home.

This time when the Tingle came, I rubbed my elbow and got up to look through the window to see if there was any mist, but there wasn't. It was just as sunny as it had been before, and the houses opposite were exactly the same as usual.

"What are you looking at?" Pete asked.

"I won't be a minute," I said, and I ran to look outside. Pete ran after me, and he was standing right beside me as I opened the front door...

But there was still no mist.

And there wasn't a path, either.

We were looking straight into the hallway of Stargirl Academy!

I gasped, and Pete let out a startled squeak. "What's this place? What's happened?"

"Erm…" I said. I didn't know what to do. I couldn't push Pete back inside our house and run away from him, but what would Fairy Mary McBee say if I came to lessons with my five-year-old brother?

Pete grabbed my hand. "Come on, Sophie. Let's go and find out!" And he pulled me down the hallway towards the door at the end – the door I knew would lead into the workroom.

"Hang on a minute," I said, but it was too late. Pete had let go of my hand and was already turning the handle.

"OOOOOH! Sophie, LOOK! It's a magic place – come and see!"

# Chapter Two

I hurried after my little brother and found him standing in the middle of the workroom with his eyes wide and his mouth open. He was staring at Fairy Fifibelle Lee. She's one of our teachers, and the only one that actually looks like a fairy. She has little glimmering wings, her clothes seem to float around her and her long white hair drifts this way and that as if she's always surrounded by a breeze.

"What a dear sweet boy," she cooed, and then she saw me. "Is this your little brother, Sophie darling?"

I nodded. "I'm so sorry ... I didn't mean to bring him, but—"

Fairy Fifibelle held up her hand. "I'm delighted he's here. Precious boy, would you like a biscuit?"

Pete beamed at her. "Yes," he said, and then remembered. "Yes, PLEASE!"

I looked around as Fairy Fifibelle Lee walked towards the shelves that lined the walls. "Where are the other Stargirls?" I asked. "Am I the first to arrive?"

"You are. And you may well be the only one here today, unless Fairy Fifibelle Lee can remember where she put my wand." Miss Scritch marched into the room, and she did NOT look happy.

Pete had climbed up on a chair and was sitting at the table, but when he saw Miss Scritch's face he scrambled down as fast as he could and ran to hide behind me.

"I don't like her, Sophie," he whispered,

but Miss Scritch heard him.

"What's THAT?" she asked. "A BOY?"

"Please, Miss Scritch," I said, "this is my little brother, Pete."

Miss Scritch peered at what she could see of Pete, who was hanging on to my leg. "H'm. Well, I don't suppose he'll do any harm. Does he like aeroplanes?"

Pete appeared like a jack-in-a-box. "I LOVE aeroplanes!" He gave Fairy Fifibelle Lee a quick look. "And I like biscuits too."

Miss Scritch raised an eyebrow, and looked enquiringly at Fairy Fifibelle. "Do you know where the biscuits are? Or have you lost those as well?"

Fairy Fifibelle didn't hear. She was pulling things off the shelves, and peering into the cupboards underneath. The cupboards were jam-packed with bulging paper packages and boxes tied up with different colours of ribbon, and every single shelf was piled high with jars and bottles and books and all kinds of strange bits and pieces. You could

25

never say that the Academy was a tidy place.

"Still looking for my wand, I suppose," Miss Scritch said sourly. She turned back to Pete, and waved her hand. At once, the most glorious shiny red aeroplane flew over his head, circled twice and landed on the workroom table.

Pete's face positively glowed. He looked at the plane and he looked at Miss Scritch. A moment later, he was hugging her and, to my astonishment, she smiled at him. A really nice kind smile. "Thank you," Pete said, and then he rushed back to inspect the aeroplane.

Meanwhile, Fairy Fifibelle Lee was moving bottles from one shelf to another and I could hear her muttering. "I'm sure I put it here ... or was it here? Or there? No. Not there. Oh dear, oh dear..."

I began to feel sorry for her, especially as I couldn't quite work out why Miss Scritch was making such a fuss. "Please, Miss Scritch," I said, "can't you find your wand by magic?"

Miss Scritch stopped looking human and glowered again. "No," she snapped. "If another Fairy Godmother uses your wand, she has to hand it back in person. It's a rule. Otherwise there'd be wands flipping about all over the place. Just think what someone useless—" she glared at poor Fairy Fifibelle— "could get up to!"

"Oh," I said. There was no sign of our lovely head teacher, and I was beginning to think we really needed her. Usually the Academy is the nicest place ever, but today it felt strange. Just a little bit uncomfortable. "Excuse me ... where's Fairy Mary McBee?" I asked.

Miss Scritch looked even crosser. "If you're thinking she could help, Sophie, think again. She's got a terrible cold and I've tucked her up in the sitting room. I'm sure you'll find we can manage perfectly well without her."

# Chapter Three

It isn't a good idea to upset our deputy head teacher. She's always very fair, but she can be fierce. "Yes, Miss Scritch," I said as meekly as I could. "Would it be OK if I tried to help Fairy Fifibelle?"

Fairy Fifibelle turned round and gave me the most enormous hug. "SUCH a darling girl!" she said. "DO help me! I sent you your Tingle and then I put the wand down for just a teensy-weensy second, and poof! It was gone!"

Pete looked up from the floor, where he was polishing his aeroplane with his sleeve. "Why is that fairy lady floating? And why has she got a stick in her hair?"

"A stick?" Fairy Fifibelle Lee put her hand to her head and gave a little shriek. "WONDERFUL boy! It's the wand! Oh, now we can send for all the other darling girls—" She stopped. Miss Scritch was giving her a hard stare. "I mean ... here's your wand, Miss Scritch, safely back. And thank you so much for letting me send Sophie her Tingle. Are you quite sure you wouldn't like me to call the others?"

"Quite sure." Miss Scritch all but snatched the wand. "I'd feel safer letting little Pete call them!" She gave Fairy Fifibelle one last sour look, and tapped the table sharply seven times. "Lily, Madison, Melody, Ava, Olivia, Jackson, Emma – time for Stargirl Academy!"

At once my elbow began to tingle again, though not as sharply as it had before.

Pete gave a loud squeal. "My elbow hurts," he said. "It hurts a lot!"

Fairy Fifibelle and Miss Scritch stared at him as if he had turned into a rabbit.

"It seems to me that my wand is NOT working the way it ought to." Miss Scritch sounded grim. "Let us hope the other Stargirls get here safely. Now, I'm going to see if Fairy Mary needs anything. She'll join us when it's time for The Spin, of course, but she needs to rest as much as possible."

Miss Scritch had hardly walked out of the workroom when there was the sound of cheerful voices outside, and a moment later Madison and Ava came swinging through the other door. They were followed by Olivia and Lily, and a flustered-looking Emma with very wet hair.

"I've just come back from my gran's,"

Emma explained. "We'd only just got inside the house, and it was pouring with rain and I didn't have time to get dry … am I dripping over everyone?"

Fairy Fifibelle Lee stretched out her hand. "Blow, wind, blow!" she said, and at once a warm breeze wafted through the workroom, twirled twice round Emma,

and left her with lovely shiny, dry hair.

Pete jumped to his feet. "Do that to me!" he said, and Fairy Fifibelle waved her hand again. The breeze circled round Pete, and he laughed and held his aeroplane over his head. "See Pete flying to the park!" he said. "Rrrrrrrrmmmm, rrrrrrrrrrrrmm."

"Who's this?" Ava asked. "Is it your little

brother, Sophie?" I nodded.

But Pete had stopped smiling. "I can't go to the park anymore," he said sadly. "They shut the gates with a big chain."

"That's terrible," Madison said. "What a shame!"

Lily knelt down beside him. "So where do you play?"

Pete shrugged, and looked at me. "There's nowhere else," I said. "Not unless we go on a bus to the big park."

"And that takes ages and ages and AGES." Pete heaved a massive sigh. "I ask Mum to take me but she says it's too far and Dad's too busy."

"So why has the park been shut?" Emma wanted to know.

It was my turn to shrug. "I don't know. It was something about there being so much litter, and nobody really looking after it."

Olivia coughed. She's very quiet and shy, but when she does say something she's usually thought about it. "Do you think," she said in her soft little voice, "that maybe we could use our magic spells to get it open again? One of us will be offered the chance to help someone today. What about promising we'll try to help the children get their park back?"

Pete looked at Olivia with big round eyes. "Get the park back?"

"That's right." Olivia looked at the rest of us. "What do you think?"

"I reckon it's a wonderful idea," Madison said. "Let's vote. Who's for saving the park?"

We all raised our hands, and Pete absolutely exploded.

"YES! We can go to the park! Let's go

NOW!" And he grabbed my hand and tried to tow me out of the workroom ... just as Melody and Jackson came strolling in.

# Chapter Four

"What's going on?" Jackson asked. "And what's that kid doing here?"

"'Scuse me." Pete tried to push past them. "We're going to the park!"

I hauled him back. "Hang on a minute, Pete," I said. "We've got to sort it out first. It's not open yet."

Melody stared at me, one eyebrow raised. She looks SO superior when she does that. It always makes me wonder if she thinks I'm really babyish. "Park?" she said. "What park?"

Emma bounced up in front of me. "The park near Sophie's flat has been shut down so we've promised to help. It doesn't matter

who gets to choose who to help today —
we've agreed that's what we'll do!"

"Really?" Melody leant back against the
wall. "But you didn't ask me and Jackson.
WE might want to do something else."

Jackson nodded. "We've got ideas of our
own."

"But Sophie's brother hasn't got anywhere to play," Emma told her.

"Lots of children don't have a park nearby, kid," Melody said. "I never did. He'll live."

"Don't you care? I think that's ever so mean of you!" Emma sounded as if she was getting angry, but Fairy Fifibelle Lee floated across the room before she could say anything else.

"Hush, my darling girls! We should begin our lessons. Do please sit down. As Fairy Mary isn't well, we've got something a little different for you today."

Melody and Jackson sat down together at the very end of the table, folded their arms and stared at Fairy Fifibelle.

"We'd like to learn something useful," Jackson said. "We've been talking about it. It's all very well being able to make things float, or to solidify things so they crash to the ground, but we want to be able to change things."

Melody gave Emma a spiteful look. "Like being able to turn annoying people into spiders."

"Spiders?" Miss Scritch had appeared at the other end of the table. It made me blink, because I'd been watching the door to the sitting room, and I was absolutely certain I hadn't seen her walk through. "Who's talking about spiders? Oh, it's you, Melody. Why am I not surprised?"

Melody shuffled a bit, and began picking at her nails. "Well, maybe not spiders. But some kind of change."

Miss Scritch gave her a cool stare. "And you think that might be helpful?"

"It might be fun," Jackson said boldly.

40

"I see." Miss Scritch nodded. "Well, let's see what happens today, shall we? Please raise your hands. I would like to see everyone's secret star."

Oh no!

I forgot to tell you about our stars ... they're very special. When we first came to the Academy, we were each given a tiny star of our very own on the tip of our littlest finger. Mine was on my right hand, because I'm left-handed, but everyone else has their star on their left hand. I can't see it very well when I'm at home, but if I hide under the bedclothes at night I can see it glowing ... and it reminds me that I'm a Stargirl, and that makes me SO happy.

We raised our hands. Pete watched us before

holding up his own grubby little hand.

"I can do it too," he explained. "And can I turn into a spider? I like spiders."

Miss Scritch paused, and looked at him thoughtfully. "I have a suggestion," she said. "Sophie, take your little brother next door to meet Fairy Mary. He might like her to tell him a story, and I'm sure she'll find him something nice to eat."

Pete slid down from the table at once, clutching his aeroplane. "Come on, Sophie." He gave Fairy Fifibelle a reproachful look as he walked past her. "You never did give me a biscuit, fairy lady!"

I grabbed his arm and whisked him away to the sitting-room.

The sitting-room is my favourite room at Stargirl Academy, even though we don't get to spend much time in there. There's always a roaring fire, and portraits of the Fairy Godmothers who trained at the Academy in the old days are hung all the way round the walls … and they quite often smile or wave at us. Madison says they can help with spells if you ask them, but I've never dared. They do look very friendly, though.

Fairy Mary was sitting on one of the big squashy sofas, wrapped in a soft blue shawl. Her old dog, Scrabster, was curled up at her feet, and his tail thumped a welcome as Pete and I came in. Fairy Mary smiled at me, beamed at Pete and patted the cushion beside her. Even though she's the head teacher of Stargirl Academy, she never looks fierce or important – just cosy and comfortable. Pete didn't hesitate. He climbed up beside her and snuggled under the shawl as if he'd known her all his life.

Fairy Mary put her arm around him. "Such a dear child," she said. "Sophie, my love, could you move that little table nearer?"

I did as I was told, and the moment the table was in position Fairy Mary waved her hand … and there was a glass of milk and a plate of biscuits. Scrabster sat up, looking hopeful, and Pete's eyes shone.

"Those are my most favourite biscuits ever," he said. "Thank you!"

"I like them too," Fairy Mary told him. "And now, while Sophie's learning her lessons next door, shall I tell you a story?"

Pete, his mouth too full of biscuit to speak, nodded, and I left them as Fairy Mary began to tell him about a boy who had a magic red aeroplane…

# Chapter Five

Fairy Fifibelle Lee was looking out of the window when I got back, and Miss Scritch was tapping the table impatiently.

"What's happening?" I whispered to Ava.

"We're waiting for someone new to arrive," she whispered back. "Apparently, they're going to teach us today's spell!"

That sounded exciting, and I looked towards the window too and there was a sudden WHOOSH!!! Something had come through the window ... something that looked exactly like a flying carpet ... and sitting cross-legged on the carpet was a little old woman dressed all in black. The carpet landed in the middle of the workroom table, and the tiny woman carefully smoothed it out on either side of her before looking around.

"Good morning, Stargirls," she said, and her voice was like a bird's – very sweet and high and clear. "Good morning!"

"Stargirls," said Miss Scritch, "meet Fairy Trilling."

We were far too surprised to manage much more than a murmured "Good morning," but Fairy Trilling nodded back in a cheerful kind of way. She was the oldest-looking person I'd ever ever seen; her face was covered in deep, deep wrinkles, and her hair was nothing more than a few straggly wisps. There was a little brown mole on her chin, and for the tiniest moment I wondered if she was a witch – but then I told myself not to be silly. Fairy Mary McBee would NEVER allow a witch into the Academy! And Fairy Trilling's eyes were so bright that I just knew she must be incredibly clever.

"So you want to learn a Changing Spell?" she said, and she pointed straight at Jackson.

"Erm…" It was the first time I'd ever seen Jackson lost for words. "Erm … yes. Yes, I'd like that."

"So what do you want to change?" Fairy Trilling asked her.

Melody sat up. "We want to be able to change people into spiders," she said, and then, as if feeling Miss Scritch glaring at her, added, "if they deserve it, of course."

Fairy Trilling's eyes gleamed. "And you think some people do deserve that?"

"Oh, yes," Melody told her. "I do."

"We'd better get started, then." It was as if none of the rest of us were in the room. The tiny fairy was concentrating entirely on Melody and Jackson. "So, which of you would like to be the first spider?"

There was a very long pause, and I saw Jackson swallow. "Does … does it have to be one of us?"

"It certainly does." Fairy Trilling sounded astonished. "You don't imagine that anyone can perform a spell they haven't tried out on themselves, do you?"

Melody looked at Jackson, and Jackson looked at Melody.

"Supposing it wasn't a spider," Jackson said slowly. "Maybe that wasn't a good idea. What about…" She looked around the room, but nothing seemed to catch her eye.

"I know!" Melody nudged her friend with her elbow. "What about a great big hairy spot on someone's face?"

Miss Scritch stepped forward. "Be careful, Melody," she said.

Melody waved her away. "It's OK, Miss

Scritch. We want to learn something useful for once."

Fairy Trilling nodded. "Something useful. I see. Well, that's easy enough. Repeat after me: *Armitty charmitty, slithery dithery*. And hold up your star finger."

"*Armitty charmitty—*" Melody began.

But Jackson interrupted her. "Hang on a minute," she said. "What's going to happen?"

Melody frowned. "Be quiet, Jackson. If you don't want to do it, that's fine, but don't get in my way. I want to be able to do this. *Armitty charmitty, slithery dithery!*"

She waved her little finger in the air. The star was shining brightly, then suddenly dimmed … and we all gasped.

Melody had an enormous spot on her chin. It wasn't the usual colour, though. It

was bright green with red whiskers, and it
was hideous.

It was obvious that Melody had no idea
what had happened to her. She was staring
at Emma instead, and she looked surprised.
"You're just the same," she said accusingly.

Jackson sighed. "I just KNEW something
would go wrong," she said. "Melody, it's
YOU that's got the spot!"

"WHAT?" Melody put her hand to her

face. "Oh, oh, OH! Take it off! Take it off right NOW!"

The tiny fairy sitting on the table put her head on one side. "Tell us how you feel, Melody."

Melody ran to look in a little mirror balanced on one of the shelves. "YUCK! It's horrible. It's really, really, REALLY ugly! Why didn't you tell me that would happen? Take it away – oh, please PLEASE take it away!"

Fairy Trilling folded her arms. "I'm afraid I can't."

And it was then that I noticed something seriously weird. The mole on Fairy Trilling's chin had vanished as if it had never been there at all.

# Chapter Six

None of us could think of anything to say.

Melody rushed to Fairy Fifibelle Lee. "YOU take it off! PLEASE, Fairy Fifibelle! I didn't mean it – you know I didn't. I only wanted to pay Emma back for saying that I was mean—"

Fairy Fifibelle Lee was looking really shocked. She put her arm round Melody, but she was shaking her head. "I can't help you, dear child."

Melody was very pale, and tears were running down her cheeks. "Miss Scritch?" she begged. "Can't you do something?"

Miss Scritch also shook her head, but she turned to Fairy Trilling. "How long do you think it will last?"

Fairy Trilling laughed, and she sounded even more like a little bird ... a little bird that was enjoying itself. "As long as it takes."

"As long as it takes to do what?" Jackson didn't sound at all like she usually does. She sounded genuinely anxious. "What does Melody have to do?" She paused, then added, "Can I help her?"

"Darling Jackson! So generous!" Fairy Fifibelle spread out her arms, but Jackson stayed where she was.

"It was kind of my fault," she went on. "I mean, it was both of us who wanted to be able to change things."

"Changes come in many ways." Fairy Trilling laughed again.

Lily nudged me. "She doesn't seem very sorry about it," she whispered.

I'd been thinking exactly the same thing. "Is she trying to teach us something?" I whispered back.

"Of course she is." Miss Scritch was right behind us, and we jumped.

Fairy Trilling noticed, and she looked amused. "What would you like me to do?" she asked. "You're Sophie and Lily, I believe. What spell would you like to learn?"

I felt nervous. What if I got it wrong, like Melody? I thought as quickly as I could, but before I could suggest anything, Lily said, "I know! A spell to make people feel happy."

Fairy Trilling gave her an approving nod. "A good choice. Would that be acceptable, Miss Scritch?"

"The girls are only meant to learn one spell a day," Miss Scritch said doubtfully.

"We'd have to ask Fairy Mary McBee."

Fairy Fifibelle Lee clapped her hands. "But a Happifying Spell would be such fun!"

"If you think it'll make ME happy, it won't." Melody was sitting at the table, her head in her hands. "I'll NEVER be happy until this horrid thing's gone." A sudden

thought seemed to strike her, and she gave a little wail. "It won't be there when I go home, will it?"

"That," said Fairy Trilling, "will depend on you."

Melody wailed again, and Jackson put her arm round her. Olivia stroked her back, and Madison leant across the table. "It'll be OK, Melody. I'm sure it will."

"That's right," Ava agreed.

Emma hesitated, but then she nodded.

Fairy Trilling's bright little eyes twinkled. "There, Melody. See how your friends are looking after you … even Emma wishes you well."

Melody pulled out her hankie and blew her nose. "I suppose I should say I'm sorry," she said. "Sorry, Emma. I can't say I didn't mean to put a spot on your chin, because I

59

did, but I shouldn't have. It wasn't very nice of me." She blew her nose again.

Jackson looked at Melody, and then at Fairy Trilling. "Shouldn't Melody's spot have disappeared?" she asked. "I mean, she's said she's sorry. Isn't that how it works?"

Fairy Trilling shook her head. "Spells and wishes are never as simple as you might think, Jackson. Now, shall I teach you the Happifying Spell, or not?"

"ATCHOOO!"

Fairy Mary McBee was standing in the doorway, her blue shawl wrapped round her. "Good morning, my dears. I'm so sorry that I wasn't here to greet you. I've had SUCH a horrid cold, but it does feel as if it's beginning to get better now. I've had the best possible company to cheer me up!"

Pete appeared beside her, holding his

aeroplane in one hand and a chocolate biscuit in the other. "We've been flying my areoplane," he announced. "We've had FUN! Look, Sophie! I can fly it all by my own!" He threw the plane into the air, and it circled the room before landing neatly back in his hand. "See? You just have to do Very Hard Thinking! Fairy Mary says I'm ace at it!"

Fairy Mary beamed at my little brother. "Very well done, dear. But our Stargirls must decide who they would like to help today. Lily, would you bring me my golden wand? It's time for the Spin."

Pete turned to me. "What's a spin?"

"It's magic," I whispered. "Fairy Mary spins the wand, and whoever it points at gets to choose what we do for the rest of the day."

My little brother looked hopeful. "Is that when we go to the park?"

"Maybe," I said. "Wait and see. Look, over there!"

Pete watched Lily carefully unhook the Golden Wand from where it was hanging on the wall, and put it down on the table.

"That isn't a wand," he said.

I put my finger on my lips. "Sh!"

Fairy Mary smiled at Lily, but before she could say a word, Melody gave a dramatic scream and flung herself at our head teacher's feet. "Fairy Mary, PLEASE help me before you do the Spin. I can't go round looking like this! It's HORRIBLE!"

Pete looked at Melody with interest. "It's only a spot," he told her. "Sophie gets spots too. She doesn't get green ones, though."

Jackson glared at him. "You're not making Melody feel any better," she said. "You shouldn't be here anyway. Little kids!" And she snorted before she helped Melody get back up.

Fairy Mary leant forward and patted Melody's hand. "Give it a little time," she said, and then she turned to Fairy Trilling. "Thank you so much for your lesson, Birdie dear. I have to admit that it wasn't quite what I had in mind, but I'm sure it will come in useful for the girls. Would you care for a cup of tea before you go?"

Fairy Trilling laughed, and blew Fairy Mary a kiss. "Always the schoolteacher," she said, but she didn't say it in a nasty way. "Do call on me again. Your girls are delightful! Goodbye, children. Be good for Fairy Mary!" Then she pulled up the sides of her magic carpet, and whizzed out of the window.

As Fairy Trilling disappeared, I found myself wondering again about that strange little mole on her chin, and the way it had vanished. Had I just imagined it was there before? Was it something I should remember?

# Chapter Seven

Pete stared after Fairy Trilling, his mouth open in disbelief. "She FLEW!" he said.

"So she did," said Fairy Mary. "Now, things have been a little out of order today, so I suggest we try and get back to our normal routine."

"We haven't learned a spell yet," Ava said. "Well, we know the armitty-charmitty one, but it's not like the other spells you've showed us."

Madison grinned. "I really like Floating and Solidifying," she said. "They're great!"

Miss Scritch shook her head. "Only one spell per lesson," she said.

"But that's not fair." Jackson scowled.

"None of the rest of us wants spots, thank you very much."

"And that spell was HORRIBLE!" Melody was scowling too.

Sometimes I wonder why Jackson and Melody are at Stargirl Academy. They can be really helpful, but at other times they're grumpy and cross about everything. When we first arrived, they insisted on being a team of two, and not joining our Team Starlight. I wondered if Fairy Mary might get angry with them, but she was her usual smiling self. Fairy Fifibelle Lee was smiling as well. Only Miss Scritch looked sour, but then she often does.

"The Sliding Spell will be a challenge for you," Fairy Mary said. "There may well be different ways to use it."

"SLIDING Spell?" We stared at her.

"It's one of the Shining Spells," she went on. "It works in a different way to Floating and Solidifying." She settled herself on the nearest chair. "We'll have the Spin now. Pete, my dear, come and sit next to me. We're going to do something very special, so you must be quiet and watch carefully."

Pete nodded, and climbed onto the chair next to Fairy Mary. Our head teacher waited until we were all sitting around the table, then leaned forward and set the wand spinning. It began to glow, and there was a faint humming sound as it whirled round and round. The room gradually darkened until the only light came from the flickering Golden Wand, and we all held our breath.

"Spin, spin, spin," Fairy Mary sang. "Who will choose? Who will it be? Whose destiny will change today? Spin, wand, spin… "

The Golden Wand seemed to spin for ages and ages, but at last it began to slow. As the golden light faded, so the room grew brighter, and I could see everyone watching the wand intently. I was SO hoping it would point at me or one of the others in Team Starlight! But it didn't. It hesitated, then twitched, twitched again – and stopped. It was pointing straight at Jackson.

"YES!" Jackson punched the air. "I've been waiting for AGES! And today's the best day it could have happened! I know EXACTLY what I want to do!"

Pete beamed at her. "Get my park opened!"

"What?" Jackson looked blank, then frowned. "No. I don't care about any parks. I'm going to help my mum. She works in a

council office, and last week something went wrong. She won't tell me what happened, but now her boss is being horrible to her. I've heard her crying at night, and I know she's scared she'll lose her job ... so I want to make it better for her."

"But what about ME?" Melody wailed. "Aren't you going to help me?"

Jackson looked at her friend and gave a little shrug. "Honestly, Melody – I'm sure it'll be OK about your spot. Don't you see? I HAVE to help my mum! If you saw how worried she looks, you'd understand. And it isn't as if anyone will see you, anyway. As long as you've got your magic pendant, you'll be invisible." Jackson pulled her Stargirl necklace out from under her T shirt, and looked at the rest of us. "Are you going to help? Because if you are, I'll tell you my plan."

There was a moment's hesitation before Olivia and Emma said that it was Jackson's choice, so of course they'd help.

"And maybe we can do something about the park next time," Olivia added.

"Count me in, Jackson," said Madison, and Ava and Lily nodded.

I nodded too, but I didn't say anything. When Jackson had said that she didn't care about the park, Pete had slid under the table and I couldn't get him to come out.

"Come on, Pete," I said. "PLEASE come and sit at the table!"

"Don't want to," he said, and I could hear that he was crying.

Learning to be a Stargirl was the most exciting thing that had ever happened to me, but now I was competely split in two. Half of me was wishing and wishing that Pete was at home with Mum. The other half was feeling so sorry for him that I almost wanted to cry as well.

I sighed as I made a decision. I had to look after my little brother before I did anything else, even if it meant leaving all my friends.

"Fairy Mary," I asked, "would Pete be able to come with me if I went to help Jackson's mum?"

"Certainly not!" Miss Scritch sounded horrified. "Why, the very idea! What can you be thinking of, Sophie?"

"In that case," I said, "I'm really, REALLY sorry, but I have to take him home."

Melody snorted. "You should never have

brought him in the first place," she said, but
Fairy Mary McBee held up her hand.

"That's very thoughtful of you, Sophie,"
she said. "And no more than I would expect.
I really can't see a problem with Pete coming
with you. After all, he won't remember
anything that's happened here once you get
back home. It'll all seem like a hazy kind of
dream – except, perhaps, for his aeroplane!"
She chuckled. "Fairy Fifibelle, could you
find Pete a necklace?"

Miss Scritch had the most disapproving
expression on her face, but I breathed a sigh
of relief. I'd have HATED to miss out on the
rest of the day.

"Hey! Pete!" I peered at him under the
table. "We're going on an adventure!"

There was a snuffling noise before Pete's
voice asked, "Can I bring my aeroplane?"

75

I looked at Fairy Mary McBee, and she nodded.

"Of course you can," I said, and my little brother reappeared. He was covered in dust, and his face was red, but he was smiling.

"Look what I can do," he said, and he sent the plane circling round the room.

Miss Scritch raised an eyebrow, but all my friends clapped – except for Melody and Jackson.

# Chapter Eight

Pete wasn't at all sure about wearing a necklace. We explained to him that the pendant was magic, and it made you invisible when you touched it, but even though he'd seen me and Lily vanish and then reappear a couple of times, he still wasn't convinced. "Boys don't wear things like that," he explained. "Boys don't wear sparkly things."

Miss Scritch nodded. "I'm not very enthusiastic about sparkles myself," she said, and pointed her finger at the twinkling necklace in Fairy Fifibelle's hand. At once it changed into a plain silver chain, with the pendant on the end. "There," she said, and Pete looked much happier.

"That's like a sports medal," he said. "That's OK." And he hung it round his neck.

Fairy Mary McBee looked pleased. "Excellent," she said. "Now, Fairy Mary and I will give you girls five minutes to talk about what you're going to do and then we'll organize hot chocolate and biscuits."

As Fairy Mary and Fairy Fifibelle hurried out of the workroom, and Miss Scritch began to clear the table, Jackson sat back and folded her arms.

"I've got it sorted. Melody and I are

going to go to the council office where my mum works, and we're going to put a Floating Spell on all the papers, and move them round so they're in the wrong place. That'll make everyone who works there panic! And then, when my mum comes along, she'll know how to sort it out. She's a genius at that kind of thing. That'll make the boss realize how special she is, and he'll stop bullying her."

Melody nodded. "And they'll never guess how it happened, because we'll be invisible." She gave Jackson a quick glance. "Won't we, Jackson?"

"Of course," Jackson said.

"What about us?" Madison asked. "What do you want us to do?"

"Nothing. It's a Team-Twinstar special," Jackson told her.

79

"Ahem." Miss Scritch cleared her throat.

Jackson went on, "But I suppose you'll all have to come too. Just make sure you don't get in our way."

Lily was looking puzzled. "But how will we get to your mum's office?"

"Honestly, Lily." Jackson sighed wearily, as if Lily had asked a really stupid question. "The Academy floats on a cloud, doesn't it? We'll ask Fairy Mary McBee to float us right beside the office block. With any luck, we won't even need to go inside; we'll be able to see everything through the windows. They're huge – Mum says it's like working in space."

Ava started to ask a question, but I didn't hear what she said. Fairy Fifibelle flew into the room waving her hand and a second later mugs of hot chocolate and plates of sandwiches and biscuits were floating down to the table. The next minute I was trying to stop Pete helping himself to all the biscuits at once.

Emma gave me a sympathetic wink. "I've got a little sister," she said. "She's cute, but she does get in the way when I want to be with my friends. My mum thinks I was invented to look after her."

I couldn't help winking back. "So does

mine and it drives me mad sometimes."

Miss Scritch sniffed. "Perhaps I might remind you, Sophie, that Stargirls should look after their families as well as going out to help others."

"That's EXACTLY why I'm going to help my mum," Jackson said, and she gave me a superior smile. "When can we go, Fairy Mary? I've got it all planned. We need to go to the corner of Garden Street and Milestone Lane, and you can't miss the building because it's the only tower block in that part of Lowstone. My mum's office is on the top floor, so it'll be ever so easy to find."

Fairy Fifibelle Lee came drifting over to our side of the table. "How wonderful, my precious. Fairy Mary, how will our poppets be travelling?"

"That's what I want to know," Ava said.

Fairy Mary McBee glanced out of the window. "The wind's in the right direction. I think we'll be able to float there. It won't take us long, so you'd better get ready. Have you all got your necklaces on? Remember how important it is that nobody sees you – although you'll be fine if you stay inside the Travelling Tower."

We all had our necklaces, and Pete reported that he and his medal were ready as well.

"Time for you to make your way to the Tower," Fairy Mary told us. "You won't need to leave it, I hope, but you'll get much the best view from there. When you come back, you'll find us in the sitting room. Good luck!"

We looked at each other. "Aren't you coming too, Fairy Mary?" Ava asked.

"I'd LOVE to keep our darling girls company," Fairy Fifibelle said, but Fairy Mary put a restraining hand on her arm.

"It's best if the Stargirls work on their own," she said. "They'll find out so much more that way. Miss Scritch, perhaps you could send the mugs to the kitchen?"

Fairy Fifibelle Lee looked disappointed, but she nodded. Miss Scritch pulled out her

wand and pointed it at the tray of mugs –
and they immediately grew wings and
fluttered out of the workroom, twittering
to each other as they flew.

Miss Scritch gave Fairy Fifibelle a furious
glare. "I don't know what you did with my
wand," she snapped, but it is NOT behaving
the way it should!" And she marched after
the flying mugs.

# Chapter Nine

We were all laughing as we hurried along the winding passages that led to the Travelling Tower.

"Poor Miss Scritch," Lily said. "She does have a hard time. She so wants everything to be correct!"

"I think it serves her right." Melody made a face. "She's much too strict."

Pete tugged at Melody's sleeve. "She's not strict. She's nice! She gave me my aeroplane."

Melody totally ignored my little brother. She pulled away and went to walk with Jackson, just as if he didn't exist. It made me cross, but I swallowed hard to stop myself saying anything nasty and took Pete's hand.

"Don't worry about it." Madison appeared beside me, and took Pete's other hand. "They think they're better than us, but they aren't."

"Where are we going?" Pete asked. "What's the Travelling Tower?"

Madison grinned at him. "It's completely made of glass, and you can see for miles and MILES! It's like being in an aeroplane!"

"COOL!" Pete's eyes went very round. "Let's get there NOW!"

I was glad Madison hadn't mentioned that the Travelling Tower could also go up and down like a lift; Pete would have wanted to do that for sure. As it was, he was SO delighted when we stepped out of the dark dusty passages and into the glass-walled room. He ran to look out, and we followed after him.

"Wow, wow, wow, WOW!" Pete's voice
was a squeak of astonishment, and I knew
why. I'd felt exactly the same the first time
I'd walked in; the glass walls totally take
your breath away. Stargirl Academy floats

on a cloud, but you don't really notice that when you're in the workroom or the sitting-room or any of the other rooms. It's only when you get to the Travelling Tower that you find out how magical it truly is.

We were floating gently through the sky, and in the distance we could see the spires and roofs of a town. There were several tower blocks, but one was standing on its own. Its windows were glinting in the sunlight, and I guessed that that was where Jackson's mother worked.

On the other side of the room, Jackson turned to look at us. "Listen, kids," she said, "you've got to do exactly what I say, or it'll all go wrong."

At first I thought Jackson was being her usual bossy self, but then I noticed she was paler than normal.

"She's nervous!" I thought, and I was surprised. I didn't think Jackson ever got nervous about anything.

I squinted round. Everyone was looking out of the same window, and the glass tower block was getting closer and closer.

Gradually I could see inside more clearly; I could see desks and chairs and computers and piles of paper … and then there was the tiniest of bumps as the Travelling Tower came to rest right beside the top floor, just like a boat docking at a harbour wall. It was seriously weird. There we were, hovering alongside the huge glass windows of a towering office block – and nobody inside would ever know.

Ava pressed her nose against the glass. "Is this the right place?" she asked. "It looks empty."

"The whole department's at a meeting," Jackson said. "Mum told me that today's the day when they all go downstairs to be ordered to work harder, or something. That's why it's so perfect! We can mess up the papers while they're away!"

Olivia gave a little cough. "Erm ... are you sure they've all gone? Shouldn't we check?"

Jackson snorted. "Don't be so pathetic, Olivia. Trust me! I know exactly what I'm doing."

She pointed her magic star finger towards the office and shut her eyes. Melody did the same. Then a flurry of papers flipped off one of the most important-looking desks and floated up towards the ceiling.

"Can I try?" Madison asked.

Jackson hesitated, then grinned. "Go on, then. The more mess, the better!"

And soon there was SUCH a mess. By the time we'd all had a go at the Floating Spell, the office looked as if it had had its own private snow storm. There were papers everywhere. We followed up the Floating Spell with the Solidifying Spell, and the papers flopped down to the floor as if they were made of lead. Pete thought that was hilarious, and asked us to do it again and again.

"It's getting harder and harder," Melody complained. "My star finger is aching!"

"Mine too," Emma said. "In fact, I'm not sure it's working any more..."

"It doesn't matter!" I'd never seen Jackson look so excited. She twirled round and round, her eyes sparkling. "We've done it! We've totally messed it up! Now all we have to do is wait and watch what happens when the big mean boss man comes back, and my mum sorts it out. LOOK! The door's opening already!"

Jackson was right. The door at the end of the office had opened, and a small woman came hurrying in. When she saw the mess, she stopped dead and put her hand to her mouth.

"That's my mum," Jackson told us. "But ... hang on a moment. Where are the others?

 94

And why's Mum got her coat on? Oh...
Oh, NO!" She clutched at her head. "Mum
wasn't at the meeting after all! She's only
just arrived! Oh, what have I done?"

"But she can still tidy it up, can't she?"
Melody asked.

Jackson gave a loud wail. "NO! Don't you
see? When they come back from wherever
they are, they'll see the mess. And who'll
be standing in the middle of it? MY MUM!"

"And they'll think it's her fault…" Olivia said slowly.

"Of course they will!" Jackson snapped. "Oh, look at her! Poor little Mum!"

We all watched as Jackson's mum began running to and fro, snatching up armfuls of papers. She looked desperate, and it was horribly obvious that she was in a complete and utter panic.

"We've got to DO something!" There were tears in Jackson's eyes, and she brushed them angrily away. "Reverse the spells! We have to reverse the spells—"

There was a sudden shocked silence as we realized none of us knew how to do that.

"Oh … oh, I HATE this!" Jackson began to bang her fists on the glass wall of the Travelling Tower. "We HAVE to help her – but how can we get into the office?"

"We'd have to go down to the ground, rush out of here and dash into the office building," Madison said.

Ava was at the back of the room by the wheels and levers that controlled the lift mechanism. "Do you want me to take us down?"

"Yes! No!" Jackson was shaking. "I don't know! I don't know if there's time!"

"Why don't we float all the papers back up to the ceiling?" Lily suggested. "At least they'd be out of the way then."

Olivia put her hand on Jackson's arm. "Shall I fetch Fairy Mary?"

Jackson shook her off, and gulped. "No! I was so sure I'd get it right. I CAN'T mess it up now! Let's try Lily's idea. Come on…"

We pointed our star fingers, and concentrated as hard as we could.

Nothing happened.

"I think," Lily said slowly, "we've run out of magic."

# Chapter Ten

Jackson slumped back against the wall. We could see her mother rushing madly around in the office next door, picking up pieces of paper and putting them down again as if she didn't know where to begin ... but then she suddenly stopped and sat down at one of the desks.

"She's crying," Melody whispered.

We looked at each other. "I really do think I'd better get Fairy Mary," Olivia said, and she slipped away.

"Hey!" It was Ava, who had gone back to the levers. "Look! I've managed to open a window!"

She was right. A small window had

opened at the top of one of the glass walls in the Travelling Tower.

Jackson glanced up at it. "Is that the only window you can open? Is there a bigger one?" Her face suddenly brightened. "The office window is open too. Maybe I could crawl across!"

"No way!" Emma said. "We're right by the top floor! It's MUCH too dangerous!"

"Oh no!" Madison groaned. "Someone's coming ... we're too late."

A group of people trooped into the office. When they saw the mess, they looked really shocked. One woman hurried towards Jackson's mother, and we saw her pointing at the open office window.

"She's asking if it was the wind that blew all the paper about," I said.

Jackson grunted. "It's not that windy. They'll never believe that."

Pete had been very quiet, but now he pulled my sleeve. "Who's that nasty man?"

Pete was right. He did look like a nasty man. He was wide-shouldered and redfaced, and he'd come into the office shouting so loudly that we could hear every word.

"What's been going on here? Who's responsible for this? Whoever it is, you're fired! Do you hear? Fired!" He saw Jackson's mum, and stormed across the room. "You! Elizabeth Williams! You weren't at the meeting! So this is YOUR doing, is it? Getting your own back, were you? You women are all the same – can't bear to be beaten in an argument!"

It was terrible. The red-faced man was towering over Jackson's mum, and the worst thing about it was that we could see he was actually enjoying himself. The other office workers were looking as if they thought he was completely out of order, but nobody did anything.

"How DARE he talk to my mum like that?" Jackson shook her fist.

"He's so mean." Melody was beside her. "He REALLY deserves to be turned into a spider!"

I looked at Melody. She was so intent on what was happening to Jackson's mum that she'd forgotten to cover her chin with her hand. I could see the disgusting green wart with its red bristles, and an odd thought floated into my mind.

What had Fairy Mary McBee called Fairy Trilling's spell? The Sliding Spell? And the mole had gone from Fairy Trilling's chin … could it possibly have slid from her to Melody?

I took a sudden breath as a wild idea exploded in my brain. "Pete!" I said. "Pete! Fairy Mary showed you how to fly your plane, didn't she?"

Pete nodded, his eyes very wide.

"Then please, please, PLEASE can you fly it out of here and into the office? Can you do that? And can you make it fly round and round in there?"

For a second, I thought my little brother was going to say no, but then he nodded again. He held up his aeroplane, and whispered to it. A moment later it was soaring out of the Travelling Tower and in through the window of the office next door. Round and round it flew, just above everyone's heads.

The result was amazing! Everyone just stared. Even the horrible man stopped shouting and watched the aeroplane, his expression a mixture of disbelief and astonishment. He was standing quite still facing the window, and that was exactly what I'd been hoping for. I needed to be able to see his horrid red face.

"*Armitty charmitty,*" I muttered, and I held up my star finger. "*Armitty charmitty, slithery dithery...*"

There was a hot feeling on my chin. I glanced at Melody. She was concentrating much too hard to notice, but her huge green wart had completely gone.

"Sophie!" Madison's expression told me that my spell had worked, and the wart was safely on my own chin. "What ARE—"

"Ssh!" I warned her, and I took a deep breath and pointed my star finger at the red-faced man. "*Armitty charmitty—*"

I didn't even need to finish. The Sliding Spell worked straight away, almost as if it was longing to move on. The green wart was safely on the boss's chin ... and on his nose as well. In fact, there were TWO

enormous green warts on his nose, and the
office workers had seen them. They began
by trying not to laugh, but they couldn't stop
themselves. They chuckled and chortled

and doubled up with laughter, and the man stared at them, his face getting redder and redder until he looked like a boiled beetroot.

Only Jackson's mum didn't laugh. She pulled a tiny mirror out of her handbag, and handed it to her boss, who gave a massive roar like a wounded rhinoceros and sank down on a chair, his face in his hands.

The woman who had spoken to Jackson's mum earlier stepped forward. "Mr Youngman! I don't know what's going on here, but I have something to say. Those warts are quite appalling – and it serves you right. You're a bully, and I'm ashamed that I've never stood up to you before."

The red-faced man didn't answer. He just sat there.

A young man followed the woman. "When you said we had to close Greenberry Park, Mrs Williams was the only one who disagreed – and you've been making her life a misery ever since. It's not fair. I didn't agree with you either and I was too much of a coward to say so, but I'm saying it now. I didn't agree last week and I don't agree today."

"HURRAH!" There was a massive cheer

109

from the rest of the Parks Department, and an older woman shouted, "Hands up who wants Greenberry Park reopened?"

And every hand went up.

"Sophie!" Pete whispered.

I put my finger to my lips. "Shh, Petey … listen!"

Mr Youngman got to his feet, and he was scowling at Jackson's mum. "I suppose you think you're clever, Elizabeth Williams. First you throw every scrap of paper on the floor in a childish tantrum, and then you send a kid's plane zooming round to prove your point about the stupid play park. Well, you could have saved yourself the trouble. Greenberry Park is shut, and that's how it's going to stay. And YOU—" he stuck a fat finger right in the middle of her chest— "are FIRED! Pack your bags and GO!"

"I don't think so, Mr Youngman." The voice came from the other end of the office, where a woman dressed in a smart grey suit was standing. There was something about her that reminded me of Miss Scritch; I certainly wouldn't have wanted to upset her. Her eyes were steely, and her mouth was a thin line.

"Oh. Good morning, Ms Brenderby. How delightful to see you. Erm ... I hope nothing's wrong..." The red-faced man sounded suddenly creepy.

Ms Brenderby gave him a cold stare. "I came to see what the noise was all about, Mr Youngman, and I've heard everything that's been said. Everything! I will NOT tolerate bullying of any description in this department. I thought that was made very clear at the last board meeting. So, Mr Youngman, I have to say that it's YOU who's fired."

Ms Brenderby paused to wait while the man slowly made his way to the door. He didn't say a word, but he did slam the door behind him so hard that it made the windows rattle.

"And I also think we'd better change

the decision about Greenberry Park," Ms Brenderby went on. "Am I right in thinking that nobody else thought the closure was necessary? That we can, in fact, afford to keep it open?"

There was a great deal of nodding and agreeing noises. Jackson's mum clasped her hands together and almost glowed, she looked so happy.

"Right, leave it with me," Ms Brenderby said, and she turned to leave. "Oh. Just one more thing. Could I ask you to have a little tidy-up in here? Thank you. And Mrs Williams? Congratulations. It seems you are the only person here with the courage to say what you really think. Come and see me tomorrow, and we'll discuss your new position in the council. People like you are to be valued most highly."

As Ms Brenderby walked out, Pete's aeroplane did a victory roll above her head, and then came zooming back in through the window of the Travelling Tower to where we were waiting.

"Hurrah!" Pete said, and we all agreed … and Jackson Williams actually hugged me AND my little brother and said thank you over and over again.

Fairy Fifibelle Lee and Miss Scritch arrived just as we were in the middle of a mad victory dance.

"Guess what, Miss Scritch?" Jackson was as glowingly happy as her mother in the office next door. "We did it!" She seized me by one hand and Pete by the other. "And it was all thanks to Sophie and Pete!"

"Well done, Sophie." Miss Scritch gave me a brisk nod. "You learnt the Sliding Spell well."

I could feel myself blushing. "Erm … it was only because I noticed Fairy Trilling's mole had disappeared. Otherwise I wouldn't have known what to do."

# Chapter Eleven

The Travelling Tower was already drifting away from the council office block by the time we'd finished explaining everything.

"Miss Scritch, Miss Scritch!" It was Ava. "Please – couldn't you wave your wand and tidy up Jackson's mum's office for her? Just so it all ends REALLY happily?"

Miss Scritch looked doubtful, but Fairy Fifibelle Lee clapped her hands. "Oh, dear Miss Scritch! How wonderful that would be..."

Miss Scritch took her wand out of her sleeve and gave it a quick rub. "It's not been behaving as it should," she said, "as you well know, Fairy Fifibelle. But I'll try." And she gave it a quick shake and a wave while we crowded back to the window to see what would happen.

It took a little while. All the office staff were gathered around Jackson's mum congratulating her, so they didn't notice at first when the papers began to flutter slowly up from the floor. Then, as the drift of white floated towards the ceiling, they stopped talking to stare ... and they went on staring as the paper cloud began to circle round and round. Faster and faster and faster it went, until the inhabitants of the office were clutching each other and gasping ... and then the papers suddenly stopped, gathered themselves into neat, tidy piles, and flopped down on the desks just as if they'd never ever been moved at all.

"H'm." Miss Scritch looked as if she didn't know whether to be pleased or annoyed. "NOT the way I meant it to happen."

"But things often work in strange ways, dear Miss Scritch." Fairy Mary McBee had come into the Travelling Tower with Olivia, Scrabster plodding behind them. "And sometimes the result is the better for it!" She beamed at us. "Well done, my dears. Well done indeed. Now, we've just got time to pop back to the workroom for another

sandwich and a drink, and then it'll be time for you all to go home." She patted Pete's head. "Thank you so much for coming, dear little Pete. You were a wonder! Just like your sister."

I felt myself blushing again, but Pete just grinned. "Do I get to keep the aeroplane?"

"Of course, dear," Fairy Mary told him. "Sophie can tell your mother that it was given to you by a friend."

"Thank you!" Pete gave a little skip. "And can I come back?"

"We'll see," Fairy Mary said. "But I think you'll have Greenberry Park to play in again very soon…"

"YES!" Pete grabbed my hand, and pulled me towards the corridor. "Come on, Sophie! Let's go!"

* * *

I couldn't get to sleep that night, even though I was really tired. I kept thinking of all the things that had happened at Stargirl Academy. Fairy Mary was right; as soon as Pete and I walked out of the Academy front door and back into our own house, he forgot everything ... and he kept asking, "Where did we get my aeroplane, Sophie? Who gave it to me?"

I turned over and sighed, and squirrelled my way under the duvet so I could see my star finger glowing. And then I noticed something else. My pendant used to have two shining stars on it, but now it had three. THREE STARS! When it had six, I'd be a proper Stargirl ... so I was already halfway there!

The thought gave me a warm glow, and I was beginning to feel really sleepy when my door opened and Pete came tiptoeing in.

"Sophie," he whispered. "Sophie! I had the most amazing dream ever! You'll NEVER believe what I dreamed!"

But I did. I believed every single word…

# Sophie's Spot-the-difference

Can you spot ten differences
between these two pictures?

# Sophie Briggs

**Loves:**
Reading stories to her brother

**Secret fac**
She's left handed

**Starsign:**
Leo

**Can't hel**
Giggling

**Hates:**
Feeling frightened

**Favourite colour:**
Red

**Stargirl Academy**

One Token

w.stargirlacademy.com

**Stargirl Academy**

One Token

www.stargirlacademy.com

**Stargirl Academy**

One Token

www.stargirlacademy.com

# Collect your FREE Stargirl Academy gifts!

each Stargirl Academy book you will find three special star tokens that you can
hange for free gifts. Send your tokens in to us today and get your first special gift,
read more Stargirl Academy books, collect more tokens and save up for something
erent!

**3 Tokens** — Bookmark

**7 Tokens** — Star rubber

**15 Tokens** — Set of star transfers

**5 Tokens** — Sparkly pencil

**13 Tokens** — Door hanger

d your star tokens along with your name and address and the signature
a parent or guardian to:

rgirl Academy Free Gift, Marketing Department,
lker Books, 87 Vauxhall Walk, London, SE11 5HJ

sing date: **31 December 2013**

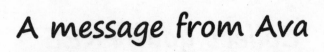

# A message from Ava

Hello, everyone!
It's exciting every
time we go to Stargirl
Academy. We get to
help people, and
that's fun, but it's the most fun EVER
when we can help very special friends.
That's what my story's about ... my
special friends who run the
best café in the whole wide
world. It's called Café Blush,
and you should try it! Cake,
and sparkling magic. What
more could you want?

Ava xxxxx